It Takes a Forest
(To Raise a Tree)

By Amy Klco
and
The Trees of Serenity

It Takes a Forest
Published by Enchantment Press
Hessel, Michigan 49745

DISCLAIMER: This is a work of fiction. Any resemblance to actual persons, places, trees, or events is coincidental.

ISBN: 978-0-9979511-8-9

Copyright © 2020 by Amy Klco

All rights reserved. No part of this publication may be reproduced or transmitted in any form or by any means, electronic or mechanical, including photocopy, or any information storage and retrieval system, without permission in writing from the publisher.

Edited by Paul Goddard.
Cover photo and illustrations by Amy Klco.

The text of this book is Goudy Old Style.
Title font is Cancione ITC Std.

10% of all profits from the sale of this book will be donated to Help Plant Trees at www.helpplanttrees.org.

 HELP PLANT TREES

TO PAUL GODDARD:

The man who chose to intertwine his roots with mine,
who gives me love and support when I need it
as well as the space to grow and reach for the sky.
I could not have written this book without you.

Author's Note:

This book wouldn't have been possible if I hadn't first read *The Hidden Life of Trees* by Peter Wohlleben. His scientific research about what is really going on in the forest is amazing and inspirational.

I am also indebted to the work of Dr. Suzanne Simard and the information both Wohleben and Simard share in their documentary *Intelligent Trees*.

I have done my best to keep the scientific information about how trees use the fungal network for communication, as well as to transfer water and nutrients, as scientifically accurate as possible within the whimsical world of "what if." If I got anything wrong, I apologize.

1

They say I can't remember being a seed—that was too long ago, they tell me, and no one can remember that. But I do. I remember growing on my mother, me and my brother connected to each other. And more than anything, I remember that glorious feeling when we finally let go of our mom, that crisp fall day. Together, for the first and only time in our lives, we started to fly, spinning around, being carried by the wind to our new and final home.

The feeling was amazing.

I could have flown like that forever, carried off on the breeze to who knows where. My brother was more practical.

"We have to be careful where we land," he reminded me. "Once we land, there's no moving. That is where we'll live forever. We must choose wisely."

It Takes a Forest...

As if we have any choice in the matter, I thought to myself, but I didn't say it to him. He wanted to feel in control in a world where our entire life was really up to chance. Would we land somewhere with fertile ground, where the sun would shine down upon us, letting us grow up tall? Would there be neighbors to shield us and nurture us during our early growing period, but not so close that they would crowd us out when it was time to go from sapling to tree?

It wasn't for us to decide. We were at the mercy of the wind. She would decide where we would land, and where our home would be.

Let my brother worry about the future. I would just focus on the glory of flight.

2

We didn't go far—mostly just down.

"We're too close," my brother warned. "We'll never thrive so close to our mom."

And yet, I loved our mom, the tree who had created us seeds—first green, then slowly turning brown until it was finally time to leave. I loved the flight, I loved the idea of adventure, but I also didn't want to go too far away. I wasn't so sure I was ready to try to live without my mom.

Did my feelings somehow affect where we went? Perhaps. Or maybe it was just chance, after all. Either way, when we did touch down, we were still very near to her.

What would have happened if we had gotten further away? I've wondered since. Would it have made any difference? It's been a good life, all in all. But still...

It Takes a Forest...

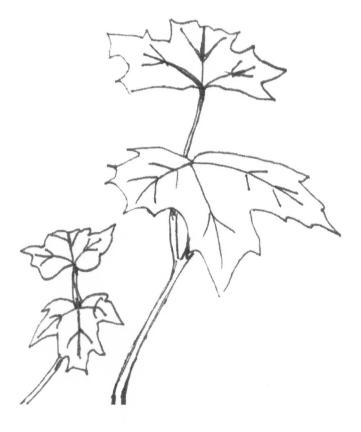

3

I miss my brother. We grew together, two seeds joined as one. We flew together, that magical flight of a lifetime. And together, we waited on the ground, waited through that harsh winter until we felt the earth begin to warm once again, waiting for the perfect moment to come out and start our lives.

But although we were together for all this, in the end, it was always about competition—which of us would survive, which of us would grow into a tree and which would die while still just a tender sapling?

I'm not sure how I ended up being the one to survive. He was the smarter one, for sure. He knew all the rules— the right way to grow.

Except he didn't. I sucked up every bit of light I could

It Takes a Forest...

get, haphazardly throwing out leaves this way and that. Before he grew a leaf, he thought long and hard about the best placement for it. Perhaps he spent so much time thinking about living, he forgot to just live.

Before long, my haphazard leaves towered over his well-planned ones, denying them the sunshine needed to create more leaves. Without more leaves, he couldn't grow. He couldn't make food. And slowly, he began to wither away.

I suppose you could say I killed him, but I didn't mean to. Like everyone else, I was just doing the best I could to survive.

"I'm sorry, brother," I told him, over and over again. "I didn't mean to..."

"Hush, sister," he would always reply. "It is what it is. I did my best. At least I know that I did my best."

4

During the lazy summer days, as I was growing, my mom would whisper words of wisdom to me, messages passed from her roots to mine.

"Don't gorge yourself," she would reprimand, on the days when the sun streamed through her branches and fell onto my few tender leaves. "Don't gulp your sunlight!"

"But momma," I argued. "Just look at all this! I can make so much food and I can grow so high—high enough to reach you one day."

"Not at that rate, you won't. You'll fall over before you ever get to this height. Slow and steady and straight. That is the secret to a long life. It's not about how fast you grow—it's about how long you get to keep growing."

"But momma," I whined.

It Takes a Forest...

She didn't argue back. She didn't have to. She just adjusted her leaves, ever so slowly growing them above me, shielding me from the bountiful sun. I still got enough light—plenty enough to grow at the pace she wanted for me. There was not much I could do except appreciate what she gave me. And wait.

5

"Always know where your water is," she instructed me. "Water is life. Yes, we need sunshine to make our food, but we can survive for months without it—we do so every winter when our leaves fall and our branches are bare. But water is life. Always know where your water is."

Then she showed me how to reach out, with my senses, to find the nearest water source. Then to slowly grow my roots to reach towards it.

"Always keep tabs on your water source, and always be looking out for new sources, in case this one dries up or goes away. You will not always have me nearby to help you."

It all seemed rather silly to me, a tender young sapling ready to take on the world. Our water source was close, a river that flowed underground to a lake large enough to

It Takes a Forest...

feed the entire forest forever, I was sure. Besides, why was she talking about not always being near me? Of course she would be. Where else would she go?

I was too young, then, to realize that all things change with time.

6

"Momma," I asked her one day. "Why do you share your nutrients with the trees around us?" I knew that, because of the fungal network, trees were able to share water, nutrients, and communication with each other. I just didn't understand why we would. "You don't have to share, do you? Why not keep it all for yourself? You could grow so tall if you weren't always giving away what you have."

"Should I stop sharing with you?" was her pointed response.

"Well, no," I replied. "I'm your daughter. But what about the others?" I didn't have to explain who the "others" were—she knew. The ash trees and the old oak. They were not her children, not any relation to her. But she shared with them, all the same.

It Takes a Forest...

"I share with you and your brothers and sisters, it is true, because you are my offspring, and I want to help you grow up strong and tall. And," she added, "I feed 'the others,' as you put it, for the same reason: to help them grow. We need each other to form the canopy we all require to live and be healthy."

She stopped and took a deep breath of carbon dioxide. Then, very slowly and clearly, so I would be sure to hear her, she told me, "Always remember this, my dear one: it takes a forest to raise a tree."

7

I thought that those glory days of summer would last forever—I wished that they would. But all too soon, I noticed the trees around me starting to change. Their leaves slowly lost their deep green color. Beneath that, hidden all summer by the green, were other colors. Yellows, oranges, and reds.

"It is time," my mother told me one day.

"Time for what?" I asked.

"Time to pull in your energy reserves." And then she showed me how to suck the energy out of my leaves, how to bring it deep into my trunk to keep it safe.

I didn't want to. The sun was still in the sky and, though it was not as powerful as it had been earlier, I wanted to grab up every little bit. I wanted to keep growing as long as I could.

It Takes a Forest...

"There is a time for growth," my mother acknowledged, "but there is also a time to conserve your energy. If you want to make it through the winter, if you want to see your second year of life, you must store your energy now."

I thought back to last winter. Then, I had been only a seed, huddled under a pile of leaves next to my dear brother. But even there, I had felt the earth get cold around me. I didn't know what winter would be like, here above the surface, but I knew enough to be scared. So I listened to my mom's advice. Mostly.

8

"How come their leaves aren't changing?" I asked my mom, thinking of the nearby pine trees. "Don't they need to conserve their energy just like we do?"

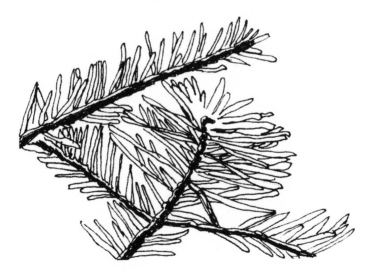

It Takes a Forest...

"Their 'leaves' are called needles," she replied. "They are different from ours. Look at them. They are thin. They don't catch as much sunlight as our leaves do. But they also don't hold the snow like our leaves would if we kept them on year round. They can shed the snow to keep their branches from breaking, so they can leave their needles on all year."

"Which way is better?" I wanted to know.

"No one way is better than another," she replied calmly. She was always calm, my mother. "We all do what works best for us. We all want the same things, after all: to live and learn and pass on our knowledge to our offspring."

And to love, I added in my head, but I didn't say it to her. Although my mother was the most loving tree I had ever—or would ever—know, I didn't think she understood what I was just beginning to figure out for myself: that the ultimate purpose of our lives was to love. And love. And love.

9

Fall was glorious. The chill in the air spoke of an energy I had never known before. Not the sun's energy, as powerful as that was. This was something else. Even now, I still can't tell you exactly what that energy is, but I know it's there. I know it's real.

All too soon, though, fall changed to winter and I experienced my first snow.

It was magical. Little tiny flakes of ice, formed into intricate patterns. First just a few, then more and more.

"These are amazing!" I told my mom as I tried to catch the flakes in my tiny, now-bare branches. "They're so beautiful!"

I felt my mother look down on me, happiness and sadness mingled together in that look.

"Just wait," was all she said.

It Takes a Forest...

10

It didn't take long for me to change my mind about winter. Those snowflakes, that looked so beautiful as they fell, stayed on my branches, cold and heavy, weighing me down.

The sun didn't shine for so long I was afraid he was gone forever.

"He's still up there," my mom reassured me. "He's just hidden now, behind all those clouds. And he's so far away, we could barely feel him, even if he did shine through."

"Will he ever come back again?" I asked, a naive little sapling in a now cold and barren world.

"There is a time for everything," my mother reminded me. "The sun travels far away from us now, but he will come back to us. He always has."

It Takes a Forest...

"What if he doesn't?" I asked her, suddenly very afraid that winter might last forever.

"My dear child, we could spend our whole lives worrying about 'what if's, but it won't change anything. It will just cause us to miss the joy that we do have."

My mother-tree was always very wise. I told myself that she was right and vowed that I wouldn't let myself get too caught up in my fears of "what if." I was alive for now and that was what mattered. I would enjoy my life as long as I had it.

Even in the cold of winter...

11

But as much as I tried to enjoy the winter, as the days stretched to weeks and the weeks to months, I did start to become fearful. Not about the sun, this time. I trusted what my mom had told me: he would be back. Now, though, I feared that I might not be around to see him.

My energy reserves were getting low. Although Mom had told me when to stop growing and pull in the energy from my leaves, I had been slow about doing it. *Just a few more drops of sunshine, first,* I had told myself.

Now, all too well, I was aware of the folly of my thinking. *Never again,* I said. *If I make it through this, if I make it to another fall, I will be the first one to trade my green leaves in for yellows and reds. If only I have the chance.*

12

And then, just when I was sure I would not make it, I woke up one morning and felt something different. Something was moving within me.

"Can you feel that, too, momma?" I asked her, afraid that I was imagining it or that it was somehow the sign of my final demise. *Had my brother felt it, too, before he left me?*

"Oh my child," my mother cooed back at me. "You have felt this before. It has just been a while. Your sap is starting to flow again."

Once she said it, I knew that it was true. How could I have forgotten the feeling of sap running through me?

"It's almost time now," she added. "The sap is reaching up towards your branches, getting ready to start the process of making new leaves. Before you know it, you will be

It Takes a Forest...

soaking up the sun's rays in your leaves again, making food and growing to your heart's content."

The very thought of it seemed to make my sap flow even faster. *Soon*, I repeated to myself, over and over again. *Soon. Soon.*

13

It was, technically, my second spring, but it was the first one I was able to really pay attention to.

And it was beautiful.

It began with the sap and the sound of dripping as the snow slowly started to melt away. Then the first rain of the season came, melting still more snow as it fell. Little by little, the snow inched away from my trunk. And then, one day, it was gone.

Everything was brown now—and muddy. But that, too, was beautiful. Not so much the way it looked, perhaps, but how it smelled: of new life and growth and potential.

And the sun! He did come back to us, just as Mom had promised! I didn't have leaves, yet, to soak up his life-giving rays, but I could feel his warmth on my bark. And I knew

It Takes a Forest...

it would be soon, now. I started to focus my energy towards the tips of my branches, slowly willing little buds to form there.

14

I wasn't the only one creating buds. All the trees around me were doing the same. And there were other things starting to poke up out of the ground. Green sprouts shooting up through last year's fallen leaves.

And then the flowers came. Little, delicate ones first. They would open up during the day and close up again when night fell.

It Takes a Forest...

"Spring beauties," Momma called them, and they were. "They are the first ones to bloom in the spring," she explained to me. "But others will be coming out soon."

They did. Little purple violets. Yellow trout lilies. And the trillium! Beautiful white flowers covering the forest as far as I could see. They were magical.

15

There was also a strange thing my mom once told me was called a Jack-in-the-Pulpit. I wasn't quite sure if it was a flower, since it was various shades of green with only a hint of dark purple hidden underneath the lid of its odd, cup-like structure.

"How can that

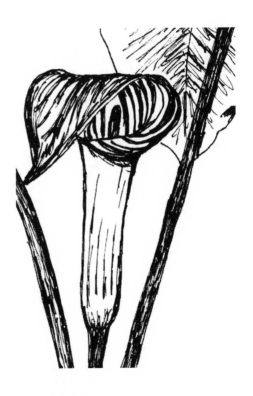

It Takes a Forest...

be a flower?" I asked her. "Where is its color? Where are its petals?"

Mom explained to me then that a flower was not determined by its color or its shape but by what it did.

And that is when she had "the talk" with me, explaining how seeds were created and how I had come to find myself in that seedpod with my brother. Something about pollination and the birds and the bees and...to be honest, I tuned most of it out. I didn't really want to know—not yet. I just wanted to think of it as a miracle.

Now, even knowing what happens, I am still convinced that it is a miracle.

16

It was easy to talk to momma—her roots and mine were intertwined. But I could talk to other trees, too, thanks to the fungus. They had roots spreading everywhere, tied into the roots of trees hundreds of miles away!

When I was young, I mostly just talked to my mom. But as I got older, I also got bolder. I decided it was time to get to know the neighbors. I didn't want to continue to think of them, as I once had, as "others." I wanted to know who they were.

So how does it work, you ask, talking to other trees through the fungal network? You just think of the tree and send a message towards it. The fungus does the rest. How? I don't know. Maybe it's magic.

The first tree I spoke to was the old oak tree. He was big, taller even than momma and twice as big around.

It Takes a Forest...

"Hello," I said shyly, hoping I wasn't disturbing him. "I...uh...I was just wondering how old you are."

"I have lived through four-hundred and ninety five winters," he replied proudly. "Longer than anyone left here in this forest, even before you maples moved in and took over. Why, I remember when your mother was a young whipper-snapper like you are now."

"And what is the most important thing you have learned," I asked, being too young to realize that this was not the type of question to ask someone you'd just met.

"Well, that is a good question," the old oak replied. "No one has ever asked me that before. I will have to think about it. Ask me again tomorrow."

I was a curious thing back then, and I wasn't really interested in waiting. Still, I knew enough not to pester him for an answer. If he said to ask again tomorrow, I would wait and ask again tomorrow. In the meantime, there were other trees to talk to.

17

"Hello. It's uh...me," I said, next, to the nearby ash tree. "Over here. I was just wondering if you could tell me what you have learned in your life."

I could feel his attention shift, his leaves leaning towards me suddenly, sizing me up. It didn't take him long. *Nope,* he must have concluded. *She's harmless. I can share with her.*

"Always remember this," he told me, leaning nearer as if in an effort to keep others from hearing, although the way the fungal network worked, there was no fear of that. They kept our secrets. "You have to fight to survive. No matter what anyone tells you, in this world, it is every tree for itself."

"But momma says it takes a forest..." I started, but he quickly cut me off.

"Your mom is an idealist," he retorted. "And it's easy for

It Takes a Forest...

her to be, surrounded by all her kinfolk. You maples think you own this forest now and can do whatever you want. But I'm here to tell you, I'm not leaving. I will fight for every scrap that I need—every ray of sunlight, every drop of water, every ounce of nutrients in the soil. And I will go on living, just to spite you all. I don't need any of you!"

I thought back to earlier that spring, when Momma and all the other maples were starting to sprout leaves, but many of the ashes, including this one, had not yet begun to put out any buds. They were weak, tired after a longer-than-usual winter.

I had worried that they might not have enough reserved energy to open up those first critical leaves.

Momma wasn't worried, though—she was never one to worry. Instead, she was the type to act. She diverted a great deal of her food supply from us maples to send it, instead, to our neighboring ash trees. With that added boost, they were able to send out some leaves. Enough to soak up light, to create food, to make more leaves. This tree had survived the spring because of Momma, even if, as I sensed now, he would never admit to it.

If that was what he meant when he said that Momma was an "idealist," then I wanted to be an idealist, too.

18

"I'm back," I said, as way of an introduction to the oak tree the next day. "Do you have an answer yet?"

"Aren't you a bold little one," he said, but I could tell that he didn't mind my boldness. He might even—was that admiration I heard in his reply?

"I just...I just want to know everything I can—about everything."

"Oh," the oak replied. "Is that all?"

"Well," I answered. "What is the purpose of life, except to learn?"

"Ah," the oak said. "Now you are hinting at my lesson. What is the purpose of life?"

"And?" I asked. "What's the answer?"

"I'm glad you asked. There are three main purposes for

It Takes a Forest...

life, each equally valid. Each tree must decide for themselves which they will focus on. For some, the purpose of life is just to survive. That is, after all, a hard enough task in itself. For these trees, their focus is on doing what is best for their own survival. How do they get the right amount of sunlight and water and nutrients? How do they avoid being damaged in the wind or by wild animals? How do they protect themselves from an insect infestation? Some choose to keep their focus at this level, but others—those who are not lucky enough to grow in a friendly forest such as ours—often have no choice. Survival becomes their only focus because, if they can't survive, nothing else matters."

It was the first time I thought about trees that did not have a forest to grow up in—it would not be my last.

The oak was silent for a bit, as if letting that thought soak in. Then he continued his lesson. "You already mentioned the second purpose in life—the pursuit of knowledge. There is so much to learn, young one, more than you can learn even if you live to be over four hundred like me. Never stop striving to learn more. It is a noble purpose, indeed."

I straightened my little stem, proud of his words to me, feeling smug that, at such a young age, I already knew the purpose to life.

"But there is another, even grander purpose," he told me, before I could get too full of myself. "To create new life. If you are lucky, you can live a few hundred years. After that, what becomes of all the knowledge you have gained? What good does it do unless you have others to share it with?"

"Like Momma does with me?" I asked.

"Yes, just like your mother does with you," he replied.

I was silent for a while, thinking. I thought about my momma and all that she did for me and my brothers and sisters and every tree in the forest.

"There's a fourth purpose to life," I said, not even realizing it until the words came out. "To help others. Not just our own offspring. Not just those that can help us survive, even," I added, again without thinking about it. "But everyone that you can—trees, flowers, animals, insects. We can even help the fungus," I added, although it seemed silly to think of helping them—they were the ones who were there to help us.

"Thank you," a voice said in my head, but it wasn't the oak tree. It was the first time the fungi ever spoke directly to me. Most trees never heard their voice at all. I knew right away that this was something special, something sacred.

19

"What is the most important thing that you have learned in life?" became my mantra, the question I would ask everyone I met—trees, birds, animals, insects, flowers. I was eager for knowledge and they, in turn, all seemed eager to share what they knew.

By this time, Momma had told me that it was impolite to ask such a direct question: if someone wanted to share their wisdom, it was up to them when and how they would share.

I listened to what Momma said, but I didn't heed her advice. I knew that, in this case, she was wrong. I knew because every time I asked someone "What have you learned?" they instantly stood up a bit straighter. They felt better about themselves. They felt proud, not offended,

It Takes a Forest...

that someone wanted to know what they had to share. It didn't matter who I asked—every one of them wanted to be heard. And I wanted to hear.

20

Everyone I asked had a different answer and every one was profound.

"Enjoy the moment," the trillium told me. "And be beautiful. Life doesn't last long, but if you can attract the bees and butterflies, you will live on in your offspring."

It Takes a Forest...

"Always plan ahead," said a squirrel who crossed my path one day. "Winter is coming—winter is always coming!"

"Reach for the sky," the ivy told me as it slowly twisted around a nearby tree. "Keep climbing up, any way you can."

"So many pretty flowers," a bee told me as it went buzzing past, "so little time."

"You want to find the worm?" the robin asked me, and although I had no personal desire for worms, I didn't say so to him. "It's not about being early. It's about being vigilant. Always on the lookout. You want to feed yourself, you want to feed your family? You must always be looking."

It Takes a Forest...

My aunts and uncles, the other maples that surrounded me and Momma, all told me pretty much the same thing: "Be wise and grow straight, so that you can live a long life. It's all about how long you get to live."

So many of those around me, I thought to myself, *are living for the first purpose: survival. But there has to be more than that!*

21

The butterfly told of a different story. "I was once just a caterpillar, slowly making my way through life at the speed of a crawl. It was just crawl to a leaf, eat from it, crawl to the next one, day after day. And then one day, out of nowhere, something inside me said to stop and make a cocoon. I did it, although I had no idea why. I covered myself up from the tip of my head to my very last legs, walling myself away from the world."

"Were you scared?" I asked her.

"Very," the butterfly confessed. "I was in that dark place for so long. And I was falling apart—literally. At one point, I was only a bit of goo with just enough of a mind to remember who I was. Yes, it was scary."

She paused for a moment, as if remembering that time.

It Takes a Forest...

"I had no idea what to expect," she continued. "I just had to trust that the voice inside knew what it was doing."

"And did it?" I asked, so caught up in the story I forgot that I already knew the answer.

"Well, what do you think?" she asked me as she opened and closed her wings several times to show them off. They were beautiful, all orange and black with millions of tiny spots of white.

"Your wings are lovely," I confessed. "But it's not about how they look, is it?" I asked her. "It's about what they can do."

"You are a wise tree for one so young," she told me, and I felt proud.

I was, in fact, much older than her if you went by the number of days that we'd been alive. But of course, life isn't measured by days—it's about where you are in your own life's journey. Everything in the forest has its own timing. And I knew very well that this butterfly was my elder.

"What does it feel like," I asked next, "to fly wherever you want?"

"It's...it's...it's glorious," she finally replied. "The freedom. I can't explain it to someone who has never felt flight."

I thought about telling her that I have flown, back when I was a seed, with my brother beside me. But I knew that wasn't quite the same thing. And honestly, I didn't want to taint my memory by sharing it with someone else.

22

"There is one hard part, though, to being a butterfly," she confessed. "I miss having caterpillars as friends. The ones I see now from time to time don't recognize me as kin."

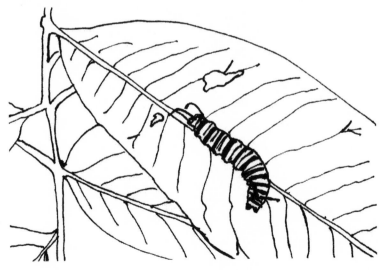

It Takes a Forest...

She paused a moment, then added, "I feel joy for them, too. I know, now, what they will be, once they face their fears and listen to their hearts. They will fly! And yet," she added, "I can't explain this to them. We no longer speak the same language. All I can do is watch while they figure it out for themselves."

23

Time seemed to speed up as it went by. That first few years of life seemed to take forever. But now, everything was going by much faster. Not in the moment, if that makes any sense. The moment was always just as long as it needed to be. But looking back, things appeared to have all happened so recently. And the future was barreling towards me at an alarming rate—summer, fall, winter, spring, summer again, and then fall once more.

The only way to slow down time was to focus my mind on the present moment. The feel of the sun. The wind rushing through me, making me dance. Drops of rain falling upon my leaves before they landed on the ground, where I would eagerly suck them up into my roots.

It Takes a Forest...

And all that time, through all the moments that were passing through me, I was learning.

24

Once I felt that I had met every thing that lived in our forest, had learned from them what they had to tell, I reached out further through the fungal network. I wanted to know what—and who—lay beyond.

"Hello, hello," I'd say. "It's me." And I would send them an image of myself. I'd get the responding image of them almost instantly—just a part of what the fungal network provided for us—but often it would take a few moments for their replies to reach me. Those moments were always a bit nerve-wracking. *How would they respond?*

Some didn't want to talk to me and said so, but many were friendly and open and happy to talk. I think they sensed that all I wanted was to know their stories.

It Takes a Forest...

25

"Hello, little one," a distant willow said in greeting. "What can I do for you?"

"I am just wondering what you have learned in life?"

"That is easy," he replied. "Life is about finding a balance. You need to be flexible, to be able to go whichever way the wind blows. Those who are too rigid, break. But you also have to know when to stand your ground or you can easily become uprooted. Know what you believe in, dig your roots deep into those beliefs, but be flexible about everything else."

It Takes a Forest...

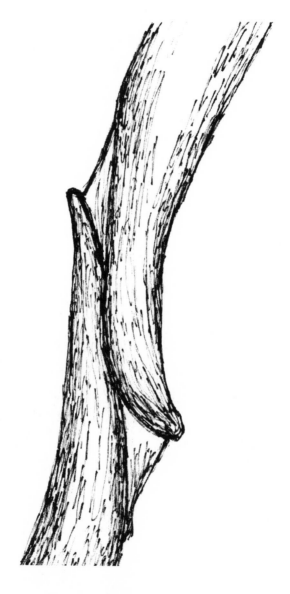

26

I also encountered bent and broken trees. Something would happen—a strong wind or a winter ice storm—that would cause a tree to become damaged. Sometimes, this was the start of a slow death for the tree. Other times, though, the tree would hang on, continuing to grow despite all odds.

"It is not about what happens to you," one of them told me. "It is about how you deal with what happens to you. Are you going to use it as an excuse to give up? Or are you going to keep going, no matter what life sends your way?"

I could tell what he had decided—and I admired him. It would be easy to give up or grow bitter. It took true strength to face difficulties and keep going anyway. This tree—despite once being broken almost in half—was perhaps the strongest tree I'd ever known.

It Takes a Forest...

27

"They said they loved me," I heard more than once from the small ones doing their best to grow near larger trees. "They said they would protect me if I stayed close to them, but I...I can't thrive like this. I can't get the sunlight I need to grow. I can barely breathe. They protect me, it's true, from outside dangers. And they always make sure that I get enough to keep going—but just enough. I need to get away from them. But how?"

I didn't have an answer for the poor trees who had been fooled into trading their freedom for safety, who had believed that "I will protect you" meant the same thing as "I will love you." Love, I was beginning to realize, wasn't about taking care of someone else, but about supporting them as they flourished and grew towards the sky!

IT TAKES A FOREST...

28

Other trees, though, were happy growing together. I spoke with two trees that had grown near each other, until their trunks joined. With these trees, their togetherness helped them both to grow stronger and healthier than they could have on their own.

"We work as a team because we both have the same goal," one of them explained to me. "When one of us thrives, we both thrive. It's all about how you look at things."

29

I was, by this time, struggling with my own feelings of being held down.

I loved my mom with all my sap. And I was so grateful for all her help and wisdom as I was growing up. But now... now I was feeling restrained by that same love. I wanted to grow, to reach the upper canopy of our forest. But there was no room for me up there. Mom filled that space, and I had to be satisfied with the light she let filter past her to me.

I did my best to feel contented, to feel grateful for what she did give me. I could have been alone in a field all by

It Takes a Forest...

myself. I would have plenty of light, it is true. But I knew from others what a sad and lonely life that would have been.

30

"Hello," I said one day to a maple tree who lived in the middle of a field not far from my forest. She was much like myself, and yet also totally different. I was growing tall and long, every branch reaching up as high as I could. This tree had grown out instead of up. Her branches spread out all around her in a lovely bushy shape.

"You are beautiful," I told her, overcome with awe at her round shape.

"No, no," she protested. "I am ugly. I'm all out of proportion. You are beautiful, so tall and straight. Me, I am all wrong. Nobody could possibly love me."

But I did, or thought I did, at least.

She was my first childhood crush, and I would visit her through the network whenever I could.

It Takes a Forest...

31

"Hello, again," I said to her. "How are you today?"

"Trying my best to be happy," was her less-than-happy reply.

"What's wrong?" I asked her.

"I'm lonely," she replied. "There's no one around me to talk to."

"What about the grass?" I asked. "Or the birds that fly by? Or bugs?"

"It's not the same," she said. "There's no trees! There is no one around like me. No one to understand what I am going through."

"There's a whole network of trees you can talk to," I reminded her. "My forest is not far away. There must be many trees here that you can communicate with."

It Takes a Forest...

"Who would want to talk to me?" she replied. "Just look at me. I'm fat. I have branches jutting out in all directions."

"I think you're beautiful," I told her, but it didn't seem to matter what I said.

"It's not my fault, you know," she continued, as if she hadn't even heard me. "I didn't ask to be planted here, all alone. I didn't have anyone to teach me how to grow right. I...I've always done the best I could, but it's no use. I'm all wrong and nobody could ever love me."

"I love you."

"No," she continued, again seeming to ignore my words. "I didn't ask for this life but here I am, and I just have to accept that I am destined to be lonely."

No one is destined to be lonely, I thought to myself. But I didn't say it to her—she clearly wasn't ready to hear what I had to say. It was as if she had already made her mind up and nothing could get through that thick bark of protection and fear.

32

After that, I went out of my way to make sure everyone felt seen and heard, that no one—plant, animal, or insect—ever had to feel like they were all alone in the world.

I met many like my beautiful maple who seemed unable to hear me when I gave them a compliment. I complimented them all the same. It was easy. There was always something about them to love. And even if they didn't want to hear what I told them, even if they would brush it off, telling me I was wrong or denying what I said, I knew it was helping, all the same. If enough of us told them that they were lovable, maybe, eventually, they would start to believe it, themselves.

33

One day in early summer, around my thirtieth year of life, I woke up to find something new on my branches: flowers.

It Takes a Forest...

"Ah, you're a man now," my mother told me with obvious pride, pointing at the male flowers that were growing on me.

"But...I always thought I was..."

A few days later, other flowers formed on my branches. Female flowers, this time. They had been waiting, it seemed, to allow the male flowers to spread their pollen to other trees. Now, the female ones were ready to receive pollen from someone else.

"Oh," my mother said simply, when she saw these new flowers. "That happens sometimes. Okay. You are...an adult now." And that was that.

34

I remember the first moment I met her. What I don't understand is why I didn't meet her sooner. She grew at the edge of the lake, the same lake that was the water source for all of my forest. And she was beautiful—with a slim white trunk that swayed gracefully in the breeze and leaves that, when the wind was blowing, would turn over to show their silver-like underbellies. I could watch her for hours—I did watch her for hours through the fungal network before I got the nerve to speak to her.

She wasn't the only birch tree that lived around that lake. She wasn't even the biggest or the straightest or the most slender. To an outside observer, she probably looked just the same as all the others. To me, she shone with a light that none of the others had.

It Takes a Forest...

"Hello," I said at last, in barely a whisper.

"Hello," she replied, and the feel of her voice caused a strange quickening in my sap.

"I, uh..." I was at a loss for words—something that had never happened to me before in all my conversations.

"It is nice to meet you," she replied, and I felt instantly that she meant it.

"Uh...what have you learned?" I blurted out, forgetting everything else in my nervousness.

"I will tell you what I have learned, but you must promise to tell me what you have learned, too."

It was the first time anyone had asked me what I knew. And I suddenly realized that I had a lot I wanted to share with someone—with her, in fact. "I...I would love to," I replied.

35

"Everything changes," she told me. "I have seen the lake go from a liquid, moving and flowing, to a solid sheet of ice, so still it seems to have no movement at all. So still, it seemed it would never move again. I've seen all the trees around me lose their leaves, until they looked as if they were dead. I have been that way, myself."

"So have I," I told her.

"But underneath the ice, the water still flows. The trees aren't dead, but only waiting. Even the sun, who during the winter seems to be all but gone, comes back again. The ice melts and the leaves grow back."

"When I was really young," I confessed to this beautiful tree, "that first winter that I was alive, I was afraid that the sun would never come back. My mom assured me it would, though, and that it didn't do any good to worry about what we can't control."

"She sounds like a wise tree," the birch replied.

"Yes, she is, but..."

"But?"

"I mean, I don't want to complain," I assured her—and myself. "She has been a wonderful mother and I am so lucky to have her so close and...I mean, I have known other trees that don't have anyone. Trees that live out by themselves. They are so lonely. I don't want that, but..."

"But now, it's different, isn't it?" she asked.

"I want to reach for the sky," I confessed. "I want more than filtered light. I want to be up in the clouds, to soar with the birds. And yet..."

"She won't let you."

"Exactly!" I replied. "She has always controlled my growth, giving me just the amount of sunlight she feels that I need." It felt so good to be able to share these thoughts with someone else. Until now, I had barely even allowed myself to think them. "I know she means well. I mean, I should be grateful, right? Because of her, I have grown up straight," I added, thinking back to the maple tree I had once thought I was in love with. "I have the chance to live a long life. And I am grateful. But now, I just don't know how much longer I can wait for my turn."

"It is always hard, living in someone else's shadow."

"It is," was all I could say in reply. "It is."

36

"But you have not been idle all this time, have you, my tender-hearted one?"

I felt the sap rise within me again. Was it because of the term she had used or because I felt she knew, somehow, more about me than anyone else I had ever met?

"No I haven't," I answered. "I have been learning. Always learning. As much as I can."

"I know," she answered. "I knew it the moment you first said hello. You are different from other trees. And you know more, I think, than your rings would suggest."

All these compliments quite overwhelmed me, so much so that I suddenly felt unsure what to say.

"So tell me, my dear, wise, young maple: what have you learned?"

It Takes a Forest...

"The old oak tree once told me that there were three main purposes to life: to survive, to learn, and to create life."

"That makes sense," the birch replied.

"Most everyone I have met—and I have met a lot—seem to fall into those categories. Many of them are only worried about survival. Some only think about reproducing. I have known a few, like the oak tree, who seemed most interested in learning." I was silent for a while, remembering my conversation with that old oak.

"And as for you?" the birch asked me, bringing me back to the present.

"I love to learn," I admitted. *And I might be a mother someday,* I thought, thinking of my newly-developed flowers, but I wasn't ready to say that to anyone yet. "But I think there are more than that. I think there are five purposes to life," I continued, not giving myself time to change my mind. I knew I could tell this lovely tree my idea and she would understand

"And what are they?" she asked.

"The fourth is to help others, in any way we can."

"And the fifth?"

"To love," I told her, simply, with all sincerity.

"Love?" she asked.

There was no note of judgment in her response, no indication that she thought my idea was crazy, so I continued on. "Yes," I replied. "Everyone, every thing that I have talked to, from the smallest insect to the largest tree, they all just want to feel loved, and accepted for who they are. They might not realize it—I suspect that many of them don't. But underneath their words, I can almost feel it. They are all crying out to be loved. I do my best to help them feel that, to help them see the beauty that they possess. And that, I think, is the most important purpose of all."

"Yes," was all she said. It was all she had to say. I knew that she understood.

37

I woke up to the sound of thunder and felt the rain pelting my leaves, which were blowing sideways in the wind. A storm. It was not, of course, the first storm I had been through, but this one was more powerful than any I had felt before. The sky lit up with lightning and almost instantly, I heard the crash of thunder once again.

"It must be close," my mom said to me, as if reading my mind. "When you can see and hear the storm as one, you know it is right upon you."

The sky lit up again, and I saw a bright streak of light come down from the sky, straight into the branches of my mother! For an instant, it was as if she was lit up, too. And then I watched her body break in half and fall, fall from her tower in the sky to land on the ground below with a

It Takes a Forest...

crash almost as loud as the thunder. Her trunk burst into flames, but was quickly doused by the driving rain.

"Momma!" I called out, reverting to my old childhood name for her. "No!"

38

Though most of her lay before me on the ground, instantly lifeless, her mind, deep within her root system, spoke to me.

"It is okay, my child," she told me. "It is as it should be. I always knew this day would come, one way or another."

"No," I protested. "No, not like this. Not yet. It is too soon!"

"No, my child," she replied calmly. "It is exactly as it should be. Always remember this," she added, even now, as she lay dying, trying to pass on her wisdom to me, "Everything happens as it should, when it should. Trust the process. Enjoy your life and live it as best you can. And when the time comes, you can leave it, as I am, knowing you did your best."

It Takes a Forest...

"You can't leave me," I wailed, not wanting to hear her, not wanting to believe it. "I can't live without you."

"It is time, my dear. You are ready. You are big and tall and straight and you have a wonderful life ahead of you."

"But, I..." I protested, but wasn't even sure what to say.

"I love you," she said and let go of her life. Her roots, entwined in mine, were suddenly empty. She was gone.

39

"This is all my fault!" I thought to myself, over and over in the days to come. "I wished for this. I wanted to be free of her and now she's gone. And it's all my fault!"

My own words kept coming back to me:

I want to reach for the sky.

I want more than just filtered light.

I want to be up in the clouds, to soar with the birds.

She has always controlled my growth.

I just don't know how much longer I can wait for my turn.

It was all I could think about, all I could do. I stopped visiting with others, both near and far. I stopped talking to anyone at all. I even stopped soaking in the sunlight, stopped photosynthesizing. It all just seemed like too much work. And for what? So I could get taller? So I could take

It Takes a Forest...

my mother's place in the canopy? I didn't deserve to be there. I wasn't half the tree she had been. I could never measure up, so why bother trying?

Let someone else fill her place, I thought. *Someone more deserving.*

40

"Are you okay?" my birch tree asked me one day, breaking through my self-imposed silence. "I haven't heard from you in a while."

It was the first time that someone else had reached out to me, that someone else had started the conversation. It was a strange feeling.

"I don't want to talk to you," I told her, hoping she'd take the hint, hoping she'd go away. I didn't deserve someone like her in my life.

She didn't take the hint. "What has happened?" she asked, as if I hadn't said anything at all.

"It's nothing," I told her, again trying to get her to leave me alone. "I'm fine."

"Are you?" she asked and I knew she knew I wasn't.

It Takes a Forest...

"It's just that..." I fumbled around, not able to say the words, as if, by not saying them, I could somehow keep them from being true.

She waited patiently. She didn't say anything, but I knew that she was there.

"My mom is dead," I said at last.

"I'm so sorry to hear it," she told me, and I knew that she really was.

"And it's...it's all my fault," I continued, confessing the feelings I never imagined telling anyone. "I...I wanted her gone. I even told you that, remember? And now...I got what I wanted, but I changed my mind. I just want my mother back."

"It isn't your fault, you know," my birch tree replied quietly, calmly. "Whatever happened to her, whatever you thought. We all go when the time is right. It was your mother's time. There was nothing you could do to prevent that."

"I miss her so," was all I could say in reply.

"Of course you do," she said. "Of course you do."

41

It was because of my dear birch tree that I started to come back to myself once again, started to drink in the sunlight and grow. And just in time. The other trees around me were quickly starting to grow, to take up the open space in the canopy that Mom had left. It was my one opportunity to grow to my full potential and I had almost missed it, wallowing in self-pity. Mom would not have wanted that for me, not after all she had done to help me be ready for this moment.

"She would be proud of you," my birch tree told me one day after I began to grow again. "This is what she wanted for you all along."

It felt good to hear. But I knew that, if I really wanted to follow in my mother's roots, I had to do more than just

It Takes a Forest...

grow tall. I had to take over all her roles in the forest—I now had to be the one to take care of everyone, to love everyone and make sure that they had what they needed to thrive.

42

"How are you doing?" I asked each tree in the forest, young and old, until I had spoken to them all. "Do you need anything?"

It Takes a Forest...

Some eagerly told me what they needed—a little more water, some extra nitrogen or phosphorous.

Others would thank me for asking but insist that they were doing just fine. Then I would do a visual survey to see if they really were. Were their leaves a nice, deep green, or were they turning yellow around the edges? Was their bark smooth and solid or were there cracks upon it, cracks that needed to be sealed up before the insects could get in and cause permanent damage? Or were they already infested with bugs?

I helped those I could and did my best to comfort those that I couldn't save. If they were destined to die, at least they would go knowing that someone was there for them, that someone loved them.

43

Fall came and I shed my leaves, along with (for the first time) my seedpods. I watched each one as it flew gently to the ground, reliving my own glorious flight.

Will any of them survive, I wondered. *Will they make it through the cold winter months and shoot up in the spring as I had once done?* It seemed so long ago, now, since I was a young sapling. Where had the time gone? I thought again of my mother and wondered if I would be half as good of a mother as she had been to me.

44

When spring came, so did my babies—dozens of them.

"Momma," they all cried out, seemingly at once. "Momma, Momma, I need you."

I had been taking care of the whole forest since last summer, since Mom left us. And I'd done a pretty good job of it, I liked to believe. But now, with all these children crying out for help, I wasn't sure I could handle it.

But handle it, I did. What choice was there? After all my mother did for me, how could I do any less for my own children?

I provided them with the nutrients they needed, what they were not yet able to get on their own. I answered their questions. And I taught them what I could.

45

It was not enough. Or they were simply not enough. Not strong enough, perhaps. One by one, they all withered away. Not a single one of my babies survived to feel the full summer sun upon their leaves.

"What have I done?" I asked my dear birch tree. "What didn't I do? Why didn't my babies live?"

"It happens sometimes," my birch answered me calmly—she was always calm. "It was a dry spring. Many young plants did not survive. There will be other years, other babies for you to raise. That's why we make so many seeds, after all," she reminded me. "Many won't make it, but some will. You will have children of your own someday, I have no doubt about that. As beautiful and wise as their mother."

It Takes a Forest...

"Do you have children?" I asked. I had never even thought about it before.

"A few," she admitted.

"And are they as beautiful as their mother?" I asked, before realizing what I had said.

"You think I am beautiful?" she replied, a touch of teasing in her voice.

I had never said it to her before—me, who complimented every being I met, had not once dared to give a compliment to my lovely birch tree. My feelings for her were too special for an off-handed remark. *How would she react?*

"I do," I told her now, suddenly unable to keep these feelings inside any longer. "I think you are the most beautiful tree in the whole world! And the most special, and..."

"And I love you, too, my dear, lovely, special maple tree."

There was nothing else to say, nothing else that needed to be said. It was understood. Although we were far apart, although we would never be able to see each other directly and could never physically touch, we belonged together and our souls would be connected to one another for the rest of our lives.

46

More babies came up the next spring, but this time, three of them survived into the summer.

"Don't gulp your sunlight," I found myself saying to them, just as my own mother had once instructed me. "I know you want to. It is so tempting to want to grow as high as you can just as quick as you can," I told them each in turn. "But if you want to live a long life, you can't just shoot up tall and weak. You have to patiently grow a strong trunk and roots."

"But momma," they answered, playing out their part. And like my mother, I didn't argue. I simply rearranged my leaves. "You will get your time," I tried to reassure them. "There is a time for everything. Now is the time to listen to your mother."

It Takes a Forest...

47

And then came the new animals to our lands—the humans. We didn't really know how much they would end up changing things. We had seen ones like them before, from time to time, following a deer into our forest. Like the deer, they walked quietly, took only what they needed, and left again without much of a ripple in their wake.

These humans were different. Their skin was lighter and their clothes were brighter, like gaudy flowers trying to stand out from the plants around them. They were louder, too. They clearly wanted everything around to notice them. We noticed. We just didn't know what to expect, until it was too late.

But too late for what? What could we have done to protect ourselves from this new invasive species? When

It Takes a Forest...

insects come to threaten us, we warn our fellow trees, we strengthen our bark so they can't get through, we develop a bitter taste to discourage them from eating us. But what could we do against these humans, with their metal claws?

They made a path through the forest, a few miles from where I grew, cutting down any tree that was in their way. Then one after another, these humans, in their wagons, drove over the plants, drove over the stumps of our fallen relatives, moving further north to cause more destruction there.

48

"Have you seen them, too?" I asked my birch tree. "These humans who have come to chop down our forest?"

"Hello, my dear," she greeted me, although I had forgotten to greet her first. I had been too anxious to talk about what was happening.

"Hello," I replied now. "It's good to talk with you again. But tell me, have you seen them?"

"Yes," she replied calmly. "There are many of them here, around the lake. Cutting down the trees and building houses from the wood."

"They scare me," I confessed. "What will happen to our forest? What will happen to the trees? What will become of our way of life?"

"All things change," she reminded me, just as she had

It Takes a Forest...

told me the first time we'd met. "Nothing stays the same—not even your glorious forest."

"But I don't want things to change," I insisted. "Why can't things just go on being the same forever?" Then I added, "I want to go back, back to when I was just a young sapling and mom was still with me and everything seemed so glorious and new."

"Ah, but dear," my birch tree reminded me gently, "then you never would have met me."

49

One day, a wagon turned off the path and headed straight into the forest, as far as it could go before it was blocked by trees. Then the people climbed out and started to walk, looking around, surveying the place.

There were three of them: a male, a female, and a girl child. It was the first human child I had seen, and I stared at her with interest.

As if she felt me watching her, she looked straight at me and her face lit up in a smile. Then she let go of her mother's hand and ran to me, throwing her arms around me. I felt a surge of energy flow from this child, flow into my trunk, circling, spiraling up and up into my branches, into each leaf, pouring out of them like rain. This energy, so strong I could almost see it, landed on her head, soaking through

It Takes a Forest...

her hair and into her again, spinning through her and then traveling, once again, from her arms into my trunk.

I have felt the movement of energy before, among all things. But this, this was so much stronger.

"Olivia," I heard her mother call in a language I did not yet know. "Come back over here. We don't know what's out there in the woods yet."

The girl let go of my trunk and ran back to her mother.

As soon as she let go of me, as soon as the contact was lost, I felt a strong urge, stronger than anything I had ever felt in my life, to have her reach out to me once more.

50

The three humans stayed. I watched them as they worked, cutting down trees to make a small log cabin. And I tried to remember what my birch had told me, tried my best to accept the changes they were causing.

"They need to make a home," I told myself, "just like all moving creatures do. Birds build themselves a nest. So do the squirrels and chipmunks. Some must even harm the trees to do it. Think of the woodpeckers," I reminded myself. "Or the beavers. It's about survival. We all must do what we need to survive."

And I found myself beginning to root for their survival. Especially for the girl-child, the one they called Olivia.

51

She came to visit me often, while her parents were busy working on their home. I was right on the edge of the clearing that they had made, still in the forest, but close enough to the edge that Olivia's mother could keep an eye on her. Perhaps that's why she liked to visit me so much.

It Takes a Forest...

Or perhaps there was something more. Perhaps she was as drawn to me as I was drawn to her.

She would sit by my trunk and tell me stories—first ones she'd made up and later, as she got older and learned to read, she would read her books to me. There were tea-parties held under my branches—with invisible fairies for guests. There were songs sung and dreams imagined. And every time, before she left to go back to her world, she would give me a hug. And every time, I was almost overwhelmed by the power of the energy that flowed between us.

52

Season after season, year after year, Olivia would come sit under my branches. Slowly, those hugs grew higher up my trunk, but the power of them never left.

"I met a boy," she told me one day. "He goes to my school now. His family just moved up here. I'm going to marry him someday."

I had no doubt that she would, since she had made up her mind to do so. I didn't know, yet, how complicated human relationships can be.

53

"He doesn't love me!" she wailed at me one day, hugging my trunk as if holding on for dear life. "Why doesn't he love me? He likes Angelina, instead. Angelina with the curly brown hair and bright blue eyes. What am I going to do?"

I looked down at my Olivia, her braids the color of straw, her eyes the green of our leaves. She was the most beautiful human I had ever seen. But then, I suppose, my contact with them was limited. And I might be a bit biased. I had long ago started to think of Olivia as one of my own children.

54

"He does love me, after all!" she told me next. "He must. He complimented me on how good I did on the spelling bee."

"He loves me not."

It Takes a Forest...

"He loves me."

"He loves me not."

"He loves me!"

I felt bad for my poor, flighty human. It must be so hard, flipping back and forth with emotions like that. No wonder humans live such short lives compared to us trees! They wear themselves out by feeling everything all at once.

55

I was hoping, for Olivia's sake, that he would decide, once and for all, that he did love her. Then, she could be happy, as I was happy knowing that my darling birch loved me.

If I had been more selfish, if I had known better what to expect, I would have prayed for just the opposite.

"I'm engaged!" she told me happily one day, assuming, as she always did, that I would understand what she was talking about. "He proposed to me and I said yes. We're going to be married next month. The wedding will be right here under my favorite tree in the whole world."

I felt proud at what she said. I felt happy for her. I was excited. I was blissfully unaware about what would happen after this wedding-thing that she was talking about.

It Takes a Forest...

56

The wedding was beautiful. She wore a long green dress to match her eyes, to match my leaves. There were flowers in her hair.

He seemed good and strong and proud of her. I could tell that he loved her, as I loved my birch, and I knew he would do his best to take care of her forever. Take care of her and also help her to grow.

They held hands under my branches as they repeated words of love to each other, and I found myself wondering if he could feel the energy when she touched him as I felt it when she touched me.

She kissed him and everyone cheered. Then he helped her into his wagon and they drove away.

And just like that, she was gone from my life.

57

"She left me," I told the birch tree, once I finally realized that she wasn't coming back.

"Of course she did," my birch replied, tenderly. "She's a human, and humans flit around the earth as quickly as the squirrels and chipmunks. They can't stay in one place as we can. They get restless. They are always on the search for something more. They don't realize that they can find more just by staying put."

"But I miss her," was all I could say in reply.

"Of course you do."

It Takes a Forest...

58

And so my life went back to what it was before she came, and I did my best to be contented with it. Her parents stayed in the cabin and I would observe them as they went about their lives, hunting for deer or working on the garden they'd built on a plot of land that they cleared. In and out of the cabin they would go, flitting around, as my birch would say, struggling to survive as we all do.

But they didn't really see me. I was just one tree in the forest around their home, just one of many. They didn't see me as she had seen me and they didn't hug me as she had once done.

59

And thus I went back to my journeys along the fungal network. So much had changed in our world since these humans first arrived. I wanted to know what the other trees had experienced. Had any of them found a human like my Olivia?

Many of them disliked the humans and what they were doing to the forest. Some, like my birch tree, simply accepted the change they brought as inevitable. A few spoke of a small child who had looked at them and actually seen them. Adults never did. They were too busy living their own lives to be aware of the other lives around them. Only the children, and only some children, really saw us at all.

It was my field-maple who had more to tell—the maple tree that was my first crush.

It Takes a Forest...

"One of the boy children climbed into my branches," she confessed to me one day. "Those branches, that I had always felt were so wrong, were just the perfect height for him to go from one to the next with ease. He couldn't have done that if I were tall and straight like you..." She was quiet for a minute, thinking, remembering. Then she added, "It was...it was so different from having a bird land on your branches or a squirrel scurry up your trunk. There was this feeling..." She broke off, as if afraid to say more.

"Did you feel his energy?" I asked, knowing without a doubt that she had.

"Yes," she continued. "It was like...like nothing I have ever felt before. I don't even know how to describe it. I didn't realize until then, but humans have such a capacity to love."

"My Olivia is the same way," I told her.

I would think a lot about love in the days to follow.

60

"I need you," my birch tree said to me one day.

She had never said she needed me before, had never turned to me for help, as I had so often done with her.

"What's wrong?" I asked.

"Nothing is wrong," she told me peacefully. "I am dying."

"You are what?" I asked, instantly alarmed. My thoughts raced. *She can't be dying. She can't leave me. Not her, too. Why must everyone leave me?*

"I am old," she explained. "Very old for a birch tree. We just don't live as long as you maples."

"You can't leave me," I told her. "You can't."

"I have stayed around as long as I could—I have stayed around for you."

"But..."

It Takes a Forest...

"I am tired. I am weak. And the beetles have found their way in." I looked at her, then, through the fungal network. Her leaves were so yellow. And there were so few of them left. Why had I not seen this before? I try to take care of my whole forest and yet I missed taking care of the one I loved the most.

"It's okay," she assured me. "This was bound to happen eventually. I knew, when I first fell in love with you, that you would outlive me. But I couldn't help myself."

"Don't leave me," was all I could say in reply.

61

It didn't take long. She was already so close to the end when she called me. How long had she suffered alone, trying to spare me the pain of the truth?

"You can always tell me the truth," I told her. "I want to help you any way I can, and I can't help if I don't know what's going on."

"There's nothing you can do," she replied. "Just be here with me. And allow me to be with you."

But she did let me into her pain at last.

"I can feel the beetles inside of me," she confessed. "They are eating me from the inside, digging tunnels. They are cutting off the flow of my sap. I can't move my nutrients around like I used to do. I can barely breathe. I just want it to be over."

It Takes a Forest...

"No," I cried over and over. "Hold on. You can survive this. You will get through it and then..."

"All things change," she reminded me once again. "And now it is time for me to change. My energy will go back into the earth. It will join the fungal network. My wood will fertilize another tree. I am ready."

"But..."

"My dear maple tree," she told me. "I have lived an amazing life. I am happy."

"Don't go. I love you," I told her, desperately, as if by saying it, I could convince her to stay, convince her not to die.

"And I love you," she whispered in return. And then she was gone.

62

Life goes on, it seems, even when it feels like everything that made life worth living is gone. I had lost my brother, lost my mother, lost Olivia, and even lost my dear birch tree.

But my three daughters were doing well, growing up as strong and straight as their mother and their grandmother. I tried to teach them all that I had learned, but alas, they didn't want advice from me. *What did I know? How could I possibly understand what life was like for them?*

I learned, eventually, how to frame my advice as suggestions. "Have you ever thought maybe...?" or "Perhaps it could be that..." That way, it felt like they were figuring these things out for themselves, instead of being "lectured to."

It Takes a Forest...

Other things, they just didn't—maybe couldn't yet—see. That was okay, too, I reminded myself. I was creating seeds in their minds, just as I had once created the seeds that became them. When the time was right, if it was meant to be, the ideas would blossom to life.

63

More years passed and Olivia's father died, just stopped one day while he was out plowing the field for the garden. One moment, he was standing up. Then he fell, just like a tree would fall, with a thud. I felt the spirit in him leave his body, just as our spirits leave our bodies when our trunks can no longer provide us with life. Where did his spirit go? Will it come back in another lifetime, as a tree or a human or perhaps a bird this time? Is it somewhere out there with my mother's spirit, with my birch tree's spirit? Do they all become one? I don't know. That is one mystery I have yet to be able to explore. Even the fungal network does not spread out past the boundaries of death—or if they do, they are not telling us about it.

There was a funeral, held in the same spot that once

It Takes a Forest...

held a wedding. Olivia came with her husband—she looked so much older now—and had several kids.

I was so glad to see her. I was aching to have her touch me again, to feel her energy flow through me, to have her hug me and tell me stories and confessions. But a funeral is, apparently, not the time to hug trees, even trees that have missed you beyond words. She was too caught up in her sadness to think about her old friend.

I wish that she would have reached out to me. If she had, I could have comforted her, sent her strength to deal with her sadness.

Perhaps she had forgotten what I could give her. Maybe she never really knew. Either way, in her sorrow, she did not reach out.

64

They buried his body under my shade, digging right next to my roots to make the hole. They put it in a wooden box, wood made from some of my past friends, then covered it all with dirt, leaving both the shell of the man and the husks of trees to decompose, to return to the earth once more. *It's nice of the humans,* I thought, *to give the body back to the earth once they were done with it. The nutrients stored in his body will help all of us to grow.*

After the funeral was over, Olivia and her family left again. This time, her mother went with her. They packed up what they could from the old cabin, put it in the back of the wagon, and rode away once more. That would be the last time I ever saw Olivia.

65

And still, life went on. Summer, fall, winter, spring.

My girls grew up. I could feel them now, as anxious to grow beyond me as I had once been to grow beyond my mother. *Had she known, all along, what I wanted?* She must have, I now realized, and she must have also understood. She had felt that way once herself, I was sure, just as I had once felt it, just as my daughters now felt it. All things change—but also, all things stay the same. It's not that life changes. It's just your place in that life, your role in it, that shifts.

66

Time marched on and so did the pace of the humans. I heard all about their movement through my discussion with other trees in the fungal network.

The path that they had once cut nearby had been paved over and now was what they called a highway, with cars flying up and down it all day and night. The nearby lake was filled with cottages around its shores and boats swimming across its water. The sights and sounds of humans were everywhere.

Everywhere, that is, except in my forest. Once Olivia and her mother left, we were all alone. The cabin sat empty. Slowly, the forest started to take over again. Local plants (what the humans would call weeds) reclaimed the garden, first. The small shrubs that Olivia's mother had planted around the house grew and grew with no one to prune them. Soon enough, they covered the walls of the cabin. Moss covered much of its roof.

I should have been thankful that our little forest, our little spot in this big world, was spared from being invaded by humans. My forest was still quiet, still peaceful. The trees and plants and flowers and animals and insects all thrived here. I should have been glad.

And yet...I missed Olivia. I missed the energy that I got when she used to hug me. I longed for contact with humans, again. Many, I knew, were like Olivia's mother and father—they couldn't see the trees for the forest. But there were also some humans who did see us, who reached out to us, who allowed our energy to flow together with theirs. And for these few, I was willing to put up with any other human that came along.

67

And then one day they came—a man and a woman—hiking into our forest, since the pathway had long ago grown over. The man was looking at a map while the woman consulted an old book.

"Are you sure we are going the right way, Mary?" the man asked.

"It should be right around here," she told him. "The cabin that my great-great grandmother grew up in."

As for me, I was shaking with excitement at the woman's words. She was looking for the now-overgrown cabin, the cabin where my dear Olivia had spent her childhood. Mary, then, must be one of Olivia's descendants.

"Over here," I whispered into the wind, hoping that somehow she would hear me. "It's this way."

It Takes a Forest...

"Maybe it's a bit further east," the man said, trying, I could tell, to be helpful.

Mary shook her head. "No, I think it's more this way."

"But the map says..." the man started, but then stopped as he looked at his wife's face. She had that look—as if her mind was far away from this world, tuning into something he knew he could never hear. "Which way should we go?" he asked, instead.

She didn't answer him, perhaps couldn't answer him while her mind was listening to the unseen voice.

"Over here," the voice whispered to her. "It's this way."

She began to walk straight towards me.

68

"There it is," the man said, when the cabin came into view. "I can't believe we found it."

"Yes, there she is," Mary replied, but she wasn't looking at the cabin. She was looking at me—seeing me. While her husband made his way over to the cabin and started surveying the situation, Mary walked, instead, directly towards me. She reached out and put her hand on my bark and I felt that old surge of energy flow between us. The intensity of it was overwhelming. I had forgotten—I remembered my desire for human touch, but I had forgotten just how amazing it could be.

After a moment with her hand on my bark, Mary impulsively wrapped her arms around my now-large trunk. "I am home," she whispered to me.

"Yes, you are," I replied to her. And I knew she heard.

It Takes a Forest...

69

They started in right away to fix up the cabin and clean up the surrounding area. It meant death to the weeds in the garden and the small trees growing up on what was once the road that led in from the highway. It meant the trimming of shrubs near the cabin and plants that had overgrown the pathways around it. But it also meant a new life and vigor to the forest. And more than that, it meant that, once again, we were seen and loved.

Mary was the first adult I knew of that seemed actually able to see us, and as time went on, her husband learned the trick, too. It was an easy trick, really—all it required was for the humans to slow down, to stop worrying about survival, just long enough to notice what was around them.

"I am sorry," Mary whispered to me one evening as the sun was setting in the sky. "I am sorry for all the terrible things we humans have done to the trees. I want to help you," she continued. "I want to help save you."

"My dear child," I whispered back, confident that somehow, she could hear my words. "You humans have it all wrong. Yes, things might be hard for many of us right now and yes, human actions have added to that difficulty. But we trees have survived, in one form or another, for over three-hundred-million years. If you humans destroy your ecosystem, if you create a world in which you can no longer live, we will still survive. Instead of worrying about helping us, please let us help you. We can clean up this world, make it a place where your great-great grandchildren can live as comfortably as your ancestors once did."

"If you don't need our help," Mary asked, "is there anything you do need from us?"

"Your love," I replied without hesitation. "All we want from you is your love."

70

One morning, who knows how much later, I heard a voice speak to me. "It is time," it said.

At first, I wasn't sure who had spoken. There was no accompanying image, as I would get when a tree spoke through the fungal network. There was no physical contact, such as the touch of a human, animal, or insect to pass the voice along. It was a mystery—and yet, the voice seemed vaguely familiar.

"It is time," the voice said again, "for you to join us." And then I knew exactly who—or what—was speaking to me. It was the voice of the fungi itself.

"But, I don't want to leave," I started to protest. "It hasn't been long enough, it's only been..." But then I stopped myself, realizing the truth as I spoke. I had lived a long life—over two hundred years. And it was a good life.

It Takes a Forest...

I had survived, I had learned so much, I had passed on my knowledge to my children and to anyone else who would listen. And I had loved. I had done everything that I came to do in this lifetime.

"I am ready," I told the fungal network after a pause. "What do I do?"

"Simply let go of your attachment to this husk that has held you for so long. Just let go of it and let your energy join with us."

"Goodbye, everyone," I said, sending my message as energy from every branch in my body, every leaf. "I love you!"

And as I released my final breath of oxygen to the world, my life force—and all my memories—became one with the fungal network.